Have A Naughty New Year

SHIFTMAS, THE THREEQUEL

A SMUTACULAR WITCHY SHIFTER NOVELLA SERIES
BOOK THREE

S. P. ICEY

SNOW PIRE BOOKS, LLC

Line Editing by @maraseditorialservices on Instagram

Proofreading by @maraseditorialservices on Instagram

Paperback ISBN 979-8-9945233-0-8

First Edition January 2026

Content Warnings

On page adult scenes
Forced Relationships
Alcohol Consumption
Accessive Alcohol Consumption

Have A Naughty New Year Writing Playlist

How It's Done by K-Pop Demon Hunters Cast

Soda Pop by Saja Boys/K-Pop Demon Hunters Cast

Golden by K-Pop Demon Hunters Cast

Sweat by Haiden Henderson

STFUATTDLAGG by Ruby Rose

TAKEDOWN by TWICE & K-Pop Demon Hunters Cast

Book Boyfriends by Decayed Souls

Your Idol by Saja Boys/K-Pop Demon Hunters Cast

One

SIMON

I twiddled my thumbs. The wait was physically killing me. Maeli had promised to set me up with her friend Kali, but the hot and snarky human had canceled and rescheduled, going on ten times now.

I'd been stealing glances of her from afar, barely containing myself. She didn't live far from Maeli and Alastor, especially once Kali found out Maeli was alive and out of her mother's evil claws. Although, they'd apparently filled her in on that almost instantly—after jumping each other's bones, of course.

Lucky bastards.

My wolf vibrated under my human skin, always on alert. The threat of that psycho Raveena wasn't gone and we all knew it. She retreated too easily; let her hounds parish far too quickly. Left them for the slaughter. Unfortunately, I didn't have a damn clue what her next move would be. I was never granted permission into her inner circle.

Inner circle.

A bunch of ass-kissing, spineless, sorry excuses for

wolves is what they were. Raveena had murdered so many in her hunger for power...and they just rolled over, belly up and begged for a bit of kibble.

My eyes rolled.

What a damn joke.

The echo of footsteps against the pebbled sidewalk yanked me from my train of thought. I peeked around the corner, catching a glimpse of Kali's back before she rounded the far end of the strip. I'd made it a habit of keeping tabs on her after the third time she canceled on me, slightly worried something had happened. Neither Maeli nor her little cat knew. And I planned on keeping it that way for the time being. A little paranoid? Maybe, but shit'll buff.

I followed Kali, her enthralling scent of mint and rain lingering in the air as she hurried to her new apartment. The two bedroom space was on the second floor of a recently restored downtown building, nestled between a couple of small shops.

She swiped her key card at the side entrance of her building, the door clicked open and she went in, relocking it behind her before jogging up the stairs. I swallowed as her hips swayed with the movement. The woman was beautiful, far more than any she-wolf I'd ever met. They couldn't even compare to my human. No one could.

Once her footsteps met the final landing to her apartment, I slipped around the back of the building and quietly climbed the emergency escape ladder until I reached the dark window attached to her living room. I perched on the stoop, grateful the landlord didn't bother with extra lighting during the reno.

My eyes followed her as Kali moved through her apartment, the careful grace that she used to drop her keys into their dish by the front door. Her sneakers glided across the laminated floors, hardly making a squeak. She kicked them off behind her plush love seat, the heels sticking out from under the thing, and sashayed her way to the kitchen, humming as she went.

I watched as she grabbed a spoon from a small dark wooden drawer. Then came her favorite tub of triple chocolate brownie ice cream from the freezer. The spoon was thrust into the chocolate delicacy, then she carefully brought the coated silver to her lips. Her tongue darted out, taking the lump swiftly into her mouth. Kali's eyes slowly closed, a satisfied moan leaking from her throat as the flavor hit her taste buds.

My cock twitched at the sight.

"Fuck," I groaned as she took another swirl around her ice cream.

I forced my hands to my sides. The need to wrap my fingers around my cock and stroke it until I coat her window in my cum was almost unbearable.

Not now.

My mouth went dry as she swallowed her frozen treat. The image of her swallowing me, gagging on my cock as she took me deeper and deeper, stampeded its way through my head.

Gods, I was rock hard. I needed my sweet, delicious human.

My wolf clawed its way to the surface; my body shook as I fought him back.

Soon.

Soon, she'd be mine.

wanted to achieve. When your best friend goes missing for almost a whole ass year...it kinda puts things in perspective.

Why put off dreams and goals of mine when some psycho could snatch my ass with a promise of a dance with death?

No thanks.

So, while I waited on two latest manuscripts to come back from developmental edits from my editors, I'm chasing the whole female bodybuilding dream of mine. Coach-free and completely winging it. For the hell of it, because, why the hell not?

It helps that Maeli and her muscly panther-man are training with me. Maeli practically jumped for joy when I told her. Alastor was just happy to see her happy and excited about something. After the little situation with the mother from hell, in my opinion—literally—it really took a toll on her. Neither of us are the most socially inclined individuals, but we'd always go out together, get coffee, hit up a movie, work out at the gym, pack orders for her shop together, or bounce story ideas off one another.

After Rat...no...Raveena, Maeli wouldn't even leave her house. Alastor—bless that man—was running around for her. He took care of her, the girl who never accepted from anyone and always put others first. She'd finally found her match, someone to take care of her the way she took care of everyone else. He texted me one morning, asking me to come over. No explanation, so I went running.

I barged in and she was curled up on her couch, head tucked in, arms around her knees. Alastor sat with her and looked up. Worried tears pricked his eyes. He rubbed her shoulders and told her I was there. She looked up, her cheeks sunken in, bags under her eyes. She looked awful.

So, my ass blurted out, with a painfully forced smile, that I was competing and needed a buddy and some cheerleaders. Somehow, that pulled her out of it. No fucking idea how, but she lurched up, squealing, tears bounced from her eyes and her arms shot around me, wrapping me in a deathgrip of a hug. My eyes bugged out of my head at the whiplash and I caught Alastor mouthing a silent thank you.

And ever since then, she was out in the world again. Okay, mostly just the gym, but I'd take it.

Now, if only I could get her to come over to my place. Maybe she could toss some magic around and fix the damn place. I never asked her to show off any of her little magic tricks, made a point to avoid it usually, given her witchiness being a big ol' target on her back...but desperate times called for desperate measures.

I eyed what remained of my nearly melted ice cream. I wanted more.

Hell, I wanted to plunge myself in an icey bathtub.

Realistically...not gonna happen. I hated the cold. Typical? Maybe, but I was beyond the point of caring. I left that 'I'm not like other girls' bullcrap to my teenage years. I was thirty-one and in no way trying to act all cool about something I couldn't stand.

On the flip side...the heat was really starting to grind my gears.

I groaned, "Oh, for fucks sake," and tossed my final container of chocolatey goodness into the bin on the edge of my kitchen before plopping onto my love seat, my sore feet on my sleek black coffee table. I slipped my phone from my pants pocket and unlocked it. Tapping on my messaging app, Maeli's number popped up on my screen.

Talk about good timing.

I tapped the little green phone icon on my screen and answered. "Hey, I was just about to call you."

I heard Alastor's deep timbre laugh in the background followed by Maeli's own giggle. "Well, you know what they say, great minds think alike." She chuckled awkwardly. "But...uh...hey, so I have a question for you."

"Hit me."

"Okay, it's more of a request..."

My eyes narrowed at the blank TV across from me. "What's this 'request,' Mae?"

"Don't be mad, okay?" She took a quick breath. She was nervous.

Shit.

I sucked in a breath of my own, forcing my voice to chill out. "I'm listening. What's up?"

"It's Simon. He's asking about you again."

My jaw ticked. Simon was the wolf boy who helped rescue Maeli. He'd been annoying the absolute hell out of me, trying to get me to go out with him. The guy didn't seem to get the hint. Or the blatant 'Dude, you're not my type' that I've uttered probably thirty times now.

"Maeli, honey, I've turned the guy down already. Not interested. No offense, but I prefer my men fully human and on the same aging timeline as me."

She whimpered. Straight up whimpered.

Maybe all these shifters were getting in her head.

"Ugh, alright, fine. But one condition, he doesn't ask

me again after this. And you owe me. *Big*. I'm talking major feature in your shop, got it?"

"Thank you, Kali!" Her whimper was gone instantly.

The woman played me.

Sneaky little witch.

I shook my head, a frustrated laugh slipped between my lips. "Major feature, Maeli. And talk my projects up to those publishers you have in your pocket, please."

"Always do, hun!" she sang. "I'll send over his new number!"

So, the son of a bitch told her I blocked his old one.

"Great!" I said, my teeth clenched.

This better get him off my back so he can chase some other tail.

Three

SIMON

A few nights passed, but my routine was pretty much the same: followed my mate to her apartment, and watched her from the fire escape outside her kitchen window. Fight the very animalistic urge to jerk off while she wrapped her juicy lips around her various nightly snacks, fantasizing my cock shoved in her mouth, the head rocking against the back of her throat. Then fall asleep against the cold metal grate with some major blue balls. Damn near literal, too, with how godsdamned cold it had gotten.

But watching over her, making sure those sorry excuses for wolves that bitch had under her thumb left her alone, was well worth it. Knowing the others, what they'd do to her if they got their paws on her...

A growl vibrated in my throat.

I'd be damned if I'd let them get anywhere near her. I wouldn't be so clumsy as Alastor had been with his mate. No hate toward the guy, but damn, did he drop the mouse on that one.

I wouldn't be letting my mate out of my sight. Even for a moment.

Which brought me to where I sat, hunched over, and hiding in Kali's bedroom closet, watching her through the dark slats in the narrow door. Like some rich guy's daughter hiding from a swarm of undead pirates. Bigger closet, though. The damned thing was a walk-in, the very definition of the phrase and easily the size of her spare-room-turned office. Her clothes lined every inch of it, shoes too, including a couple of strappy stilettos I'd love to have draped over my shoulders.

My stomach knotted, twisted with the dirty little image. My wolf groaned in the back of my head.

Alright, alright. I'll cool it. Down, boy.

Kali had walked in just seconds before, clad in her workout gear. This time, it was some type of oversized hoodie that cut off just below her chest. The band of her sports bra peeked out from underneath, leaving her stomach exposed and glistening in her bedroom lights. The leggings she wore hugged her thighs, hips, and ass almost *too* perfectly. Wherever she got her clothes, I was buying the place the moment she was mine. I had money to burn, and to hell if I wasn't going to spend it all on her.

Fucking hell.

My cock strained against my jeans as she waltzed toward my hiding space. I pushed back, scrambling to find somewhere to hide.

Bingo.

Her dresser was wedged in the back, with just enough space for me to duck behind. So, that was what I did. Just in the knick of time. The closet door opened, shedding the light from her room across the place. I held my breath as I peeked around the edge. She stripped down, tossing her clothes toward a hamper next to the door.

My mouth fell open.

Holy hell.

Saliva pooled, my wolf breaking the surface as I started panting.

I thought she was stunning before...but Gods...she...Kali was a Goddess.

My wolf fought, trying to rip through my human skin, needing to claim her, mark her. Make her mine, ours.

Not. Now.

I ground my teeth together, using the full extent of my strength to hold him back. I wasn't going to ruin my chances by letting him run rampant. Blood rushed in my ears, my heart thundered in my chest while heat traveled the length of my trembling body.

I was on the verge of losing it.

I couldn't be here. Not like this.

If I shifted now...she'd see me.

I wouldn't get another chance. Maeli and Alastor would find out. I'd be banned from my mate. They wouldn't let me out of their sight. And Kali would be too disgusted to even give me a shot.

Hell. I saw her little collection under her bed. She'd probably just *shoot* me. Then what? Not exactly the shot I was hoping for.

Taken out by my mate.

The godsdamned irony.

I snorted.

And caught my fuck up too late.

Kali's head whirled around, eyes narrowed. I dipped behind the dresser, cursing myself for being so stupid.

I was cooked.

Her footsteps got louder as she closed in. I had *seconds*.

My eyes squeezed shut.

Fuck. Fuck. Fuck.

Pop music blasted my ears.

"Shit," Kali swore, fumbling. Her footsteps retreated, pounding against her floor and out of her closet. There was a fast tap against a screen.

"Hello?" Kali said breathlessly.

Save by the bell. Holy shit.

I snuck a quick glance. Her back was turned and on the other side of her room.

Now's my chance.

I crept forward and was almost to the exit when she turned around. I ducked, hiding underneath a rack of shirts and hoodies, tucking my feet flush against the wall at my back.

Her voice carried—the calm before the storm. She said a simple, "Thank you." Silence followed as her phone hit her bed with a thud.

And then pure chaos.

Screams and squeals bounced off of the walls.

"Oh, my God!! I did it! I did it!" Her bare feet fluttered against her floorboards. Within seconds, they bounded across her room, back toward my hiding spot. Her arm reached in blindly and yanked a fresh shirt from a hanger to my left, along with a hoodie. Sweatpants were pulled from across the way. Fabric swished as she dove into them and bolted out the bedroom door, slipping her feet into a pair of tennis shoes as she went.

The metal clink of her keys told me she was well on her way out the front door. So, I booked it, not even bothering to check if the coast was clear. Her window flew up with a breeze and I hauled my ass over the window sill.

My grip caught me before I went plummeting face-first to the cement down below. Could I survive that? Yeah, but I'd be pretty banged up for a few hours, and with my pretty little mate on a mission, I couldn't really take the risk. So, thank the wolf gods for the inhuman reflexes, because holy fuck.

I hung from the rail before I pulled myself back up and crossed my arms on top of the cherry wood. Air filled my lungs as I sucked in the deepest fucking breath of my life. My eyes slid closed as I held it in. Once I released the breath, I slowly opened them and caught a glimpse of a shiny little piece of technology chilling on Kali's rumpled comforter.

I smirked.

Looks like someone forgot something.

Four

KALI

"Maeli, I could fucking kiss you, right now!" I jumped her as her cottage door swung open. My arms quickly wrapped around her, squeezing her as tightly as humanly possible.

"Would the two of you prefer some privacy?" Alastor politely asked from behind her with amusement in his eyes.

Maeli giggled as she hugged me back. "I'd love to but I make it a point not to kiss family. Kinda frowned on in most places."

I belted out a laugh. "God, you're so weird. But seriously!" I let go, holding her at arms length. "You're freaking amazing! My dream publisher just called me and offered me a contract," I squealed, my voice getting higher with each syllable. "Best. Friend. *Ever.*"

She pushed a strand of hair behind her ear. "All I did was mention it in the server. Someone was asking for a few recommendations. They just so happened to be with a publisher. Happy coincidence!"

This witch is too humble for her own good.

I rolled my eyes, flashing a wide ass smile. "Either way… thank you. Seriously, this is freaking *huge.*"

An annoying deep voice came up behind me. "Hey ladies, I hear there's some news to celebrate?"

Mentally, I rolled my eyes so far they'd probably dislodge from my skull. Physically, I stepped away from Maeli, headed to her kitchen, and planted myself in front of her fridge.

"Awe, no hello?" Simon snickered.

Ignore him.

I wasn't about to let his obnoxious ego ruin my mood. I could celebrate without acknowledging his stupid existence.

Mmm, there she is.

I licked my lips and grabbed a bottle of white wine from the back of Maeli's fridge along with the cheesecake that sat front and center. My favorite.

Maeli, you beautiful angel of a witch.

Goodies in hand, I turned on my heel, gently kicking her fridge shut before laying the sugar-filled feast on her counter.

"Kali Merry, you better share that!" Maeli chuckled, now wrapped in Alastor's hunky arms. They waddled over in their coupley embrace, all warm and gooey and sweet. Two perfect pieces melded together. I was extremely happy for them.

But yuck.

"Get a room, you guys. I'm gonna puke," Simon chimed in, his finger pointed at his stuck out tongue as he pretended to gag.

Rude ass.

"Gee, it's a wonder you're perpetually single." I scoffed.

He looked me up and down, sending a shiver hurdling through me. Almost in sync, he flashed me a smirk. As if he *knew.* "A choice, really." He winked. "Just waiting for someone special. I guess I'm just a romantic like that." An overly dramatic sigh pushed past his lips.

His very kissable lips...

My eyebrows shot sky high, my nose crinkling.

Ew. Fuck. No.

Where the actual fuck did that come from?

I snarled at the fucker. "Yeah, picking up every girl at the bar? Reallll romantic, Man-Whore."

Take that, asswipe.

"Interesting that you know that. Given the only bars I've frequented have been mostly shifter-heavy." His smirk twisted into a full-fledged toothy grin.

Heat flooded my cheeks. Steam burst from my ears. "I only go because Alastor here told me about them and they're the only place guys aren't drooling over me."

Maeli clapped her hands. "Alright, Simon...go play nice with Alastor. I think he needs your help with something." She ushered him away before turning back to me. "Now, you and I are going to chow down on some cheesecake and peach wine."

She snapped her fingers and a knife floated from the woodblock next to her sink, slicing the bouncy delicacy into eighths. Wine glasses emerged and the cork popped from the bottle before pouring itself.

Maeli grinned ear to ear and twirled her finger as she raised her arm in the air, adding some awful timbre to her voice she shouted, "To the study!"

The giant heavy wooden door that led to her office and

overflowing personal library appeared out of thin air. She mumbled some witchy gibberish and it swung open, instantly swamping us with the homey scent of loved books.

I stepped over the threshold and stared in awe as the door shut behind me. Her collection never failed to amaze me. Stacks upon stacks of books filled her library, giving that bookworm princess a run for her money. A mix of old and new books that hadn't even been publicly released yet. Books that had been read once then stored away. Ones that had been re-read so many times the pages were falling out. It was a dream.

It was no wonder she kept this place under lock and key. I would too if I had supernatural powers. Maeli was far more modest than I would be if the roles were switched.

Probably a good thing.

I followed her to the lounge that sat in the center. Two armchairs rested in front of a stone fireplace, the flames purred as we neared. A table appeared between the chairs with our glasses perched on the edges, along with our slices of cheesecake.

I dove into the oversized chair on the right, snuggling deep into the luxuriously soft cushions. I snatched my piece of cake off the table and stabbed it with a fork before shoving it into my watering mouth. I groaned as it doused my tongue. "Oh my gosh, Mae, this is fucking perfect!" I shoved another bite between my lips. "No wonder Alastor is wrapped around your finger. I'd ask you to teach me, but I don't have the patience."

She belted out a laugh. "There's more to it than that,

Kali." She took a bite of her slice. "Besides, if you ever want to learn, you know where to find me."

I stuck my tongue out. "Ew, I *so* do not need to know my best friend's mad sex skills."

Her face turned beet red. "That...that's not what I meant!"

I snickered, waving my fork-holding hand in the air. "Sure, sure."

"He...I'm more myself with him around. I don't have to hide."

I smiled, genuine.

"Plus, there's something you don't know."

"What, ya pregnant?"

Her eyes bugged out of her head. "No! No, we don't know if...No. We're mates."

My brow arched. "You guys bang and are a couple. I'd say you're more than 'mates.'"

She shook her head. "Kali. We're *mates*. As in soul mates."

I barked a laugh. "You're hilarious."

She glared at me.

Alright, maybe she's not joking.

I shrugged. "Alright, so the classic fated mates trope. Good for you, Sweet Pea. Too bad for the rest of us mortals, huh?"

She glanced down at her dessert, no longer meeting my eyes. "It's really nice, actually."

"Good, I'm happy for ya, Mae. Now, let's get down to business and kick all the sappy stuff to the curb!"

"Okay, but there's something that you should know—"

I flicked my empty fork in the air. "Nope! Cake, pub

deal, and getting drunk with the best wine known to human kind. We can talk sappy, gooey, gross stuff when we're nursing some major hangovers."

Maeli sighed but caved. "You're right." She held up her glass. "Here's to you, Kali! The next Best Seller! You'll be top of the charts in no time!" Our glasses clinked and we downed our first drink of many.

Five

SIMON

Kali's phone vibrated in my pocket. I left it at first...until my curiosity grated me.

Being a little nosey never hurt anyone.

I slipped it from my jeans and tapped the dark screen. A text popped up from someone named Alek. Jealousy reared its ugly head.

> Hey, you up?

I checked the time. It was after two a.m. on a Saturday.

It's a damn booty call. Some douchebag is trying to bang my mate in the middle of the night.

Not on my watch, Motherfucker.

> Not interested.

Three grey dots popped up on the screen.

> Awe, come on, baby. I need you.

Red filled my vision. The thirst for blood flooded my mouth.

I yanked down the fly of my jeans, my cock's rage-fueled hard-on springing forward. I snapped a photo and sent it to the bastard—thick, pulsing shaft and all.

Need this, asshole?

A satisfied smirk flicked across my face as I blocked the number then deleted the texts.

"Care to explain why your cock is out with Kali's cell phone in your hands?"

I swore, jumping from the couch as Alastor came up behind me. "Shit, man! Warn a guy, would ya?"

He quirked his brow. "Contain yourself, 'would ya?'" He shook his head. "Honestly, Simon, do you believe snooping through your mate's phone and privacy is the way to win her over?"

"I...That's not what I was doing. Just holding on to her phone for her. She left it behind. I'm just keeping it safe."

Alastor frowned. "Interesting, considering she didn't have it on her when she arrived."

I cooled my expression, shoving my hands and her phone in the front pockets of my jeans. "Well, clearly you missed it then."

He stared, then glanced down. "Apparently. Now, if you could contain yourself, I'd rather not expose *my* mate to your member."

"Maybe not, but it'd definitely get Kali's attention."

Alastor growled and his claws slipped through the skin of his knuckles.

Since when...

I put my hands up. "Alright, alright. Chill out, Al. I hear ya." I wrangled myself and zipped my pants. I knew there was no point. We were both territorial but they'd solidified their mate bond, and I was greatly out of my league if it came down to a fight.

Wasn't really in the mood for one, either. Besides being a cat, the guy wasn't so bad.

"Word of advice, Wolf. Phone stealing isn't the way to get her attention. Try being more of a gentleman. That might work more in your favor."

I sniffed but kept my eyes on him. "And what gives you that idea?" My human was feisty. The feisty ones always wanted to argue, play hard to get.

Alastor clapped his hand on my shoulder. "The strongest are the ones who yearn the most for safety, vulnerability without judgment." He squeezed. "Become her safe space. Not her stalker." He stared me down.

Fuck. He does *know.*

Play dumb. Play dumb.

"I would never."

Alastor's eyes rolled and he clicked the remote to Maeli's TV.

And there, smack dab in the middle of her sixty-five inch flat screen...was me, slipping in Kali's apartment from the fire escape.

"I can explain—"

He held his free hand up. "No need. It was expected. We shifters do not possess as much control over our beasts as we think. Myself included."

"So you—?"

"I am not proud of it, but yes. The one time I forced myself away...Raveena's hounds took her from me."

"Does Maeli know?"

"About my indiscretions? Yes, of course. Yours? No, although I'm sure she'd understand. I do not see her taking too kindly to her best friend being stalked by a wolf. Regardless of Maeli considering you a friend."

That eased the growing tension wedged between my shoulder blades. "Well, feeling's mutual."

He nodded as he shut off the screen, the remote dropping onto the couch. "However, be warned. If harm comes to Kali, Maeli will know everything. And my witch...is not one you'd want to be an enemy of, in case you've forgotten."

I gulped. "Hear ya loud and clear, Whiskers. loud and clear."

His foot connected with my calf and I yelped. "Hey! After all the slurs you've thrown at me, I get at least *one*."

He ignored me and strode to Maeli's stocked kitchen. The fridge swung open as he reached in and scavenged. Within seconds, he slipped it closed and started walking back toward where I'd replanted myself on the rug, a few beers in hand. Alastor twisted the top off of his after he tossed one at me. I snatched it from the air just before it crashed into the mantle.

I cracked it open and downed the son of a bitch. Best damn beer I'd had in awhile.

My money is on some type of enchantment.

We slugged back a few more before it was my turn to make a trip to the kitchen for the next round.

I had a nice buzz going, so I grabbed a bag of spicy

cheesy tortilla chips too, offering them up to Alastor as I plopped down next to him.

He passed and chose to read one of Maeli's books. It looked like a fresh one, right off the shelves across the way. I strained my neck, peeking at the title. Reading wasn't really my thing, but what the hell, I was curious.

I caught the title, hobbled my way over to the collection, and grabbed one of the ten other copies on display. I turned it over to the front cover.

Well, I'd be damned.

It was one of Kali's.

A spark of pride lit in my chest.

Damn right, it's Kali's. Look at this thing, it's sick as hell.

Is this the one she just got that deal on?

I flipped it open, skimming the first page. The corner of my mouth twitched.

Would ya look at that? A romance novel...about shifters.

Oh, my sweet human...you have no idea how close to home you are.

Six

KALI

"Hey, M-Mae," I slurred. We'd slurped back three bottles of wine and hot damn was I feeling it. We talked and talked well into the night, our cheesecake demolished and drink supply dry.

We settled in after the third attempt at impromptu karaoke. Belting at the top of our drunken lungs without background noise wasn't too easy on the ears. We could carry a tune sober...but when we were shitfaced...it was *awful.*

Talk about a dying cat. Fucking hell.

"Maeli," I half whispered, half shouted. She answered with a loud nasally snore.

A snort erupted from me. Her ass was asleep.

I got up, teetering and draped one of her fluffy reading blankets over her. She sighed as the soft fabric warmed her and sleepily nestled herself deeper in the oversized throw.

She deserved a rest. After everything, she needed it the most. The woman was a damn saint.

My stomach rumbled.

Okay, time to cut the sap. I need some grub.

The whole being a bottomless pit thing was a blessing and a curse. Pro: food. All the freaking food. Con: *Always* hungry. Thank the food gods Maeli almost always had a packed kitchen.

I stumbled around her library until I found the pen-sized key to materialize the door. She made it specifically for me, considering I lacked the magical punch. I twisted in the empty space in front of me and presto, massive fairytale door a-la witchy-key.

I stepped through as it opened and shoved the key back into my pocket while I strode to the heaven-sent kitchen and ravaged the place. Chocolate hummus, berries, guacamole, cherries, cheese dip, tortilla chips.

Chips.

My stomach growled. "Where are the damn chips? I know I saw them earlier."

"Yoo-hoooo, lookin' for these, Sweet Cheeks?" Simon sang.

I whirled around, irritation digging its thick thorned roots into my spine. "Don't. You. Dare. Call. Me. Sweet. Cheeks."

He shot me a shit-eating grin then stuck his tongue out. "You want em? Come get em, *Kali.*" He shook the bag of chips in the air, taunting me.

I growled. "Those are *mine*, asshole."

He blurted out a laugh, then winked. "Then come get them, sweetie."

I plopped the rest of my hoard on the counter, popped a raspberry in my mouth then ran at the guy. I launched myself over the back of Maeli's couch and tackled Simon to the ground. I had him on his back, the wind knocked out of him, the triangle shaped masterpieces in my reach.

Then the asshole flipped us over. My back hit the rug with a thud and wine flavored air whooshed from my lung.

He snorted, brows raised and a curious glint in his eyes. "Really? All this over a bag of chips?"

"Mind your damn business, Wolfie."

His free hand flew to his chest as he gasped. "How *rude.*" The bastard then had the audacity to toss the bag to the side just out of reach before pressing his weight down on me and slinging his hand to his forehead. "You truly wound me, Kali. Here I thought we were friends."

I kicked out from under him, trying to wriggle free. I grunted with each futile attempt. "I—ugh—only tolerate you because of Mae." I bucked, to no avail. "Now get the hell off of me, you imp!"

Simon chuckled, and by some damn miracle he actually moved. "Only because you asked nicely." The son of a bitch tapped my nose before I realized what was happening. "Boop!"

My mouth fell open, stunned. "You—you *booped* me? What the hell are you, twelve!?"

"Nope, I just couldn't help myself. You're *so cute* when you're hangry." The toothy grin was back and I was ready to knock the pearly things right out of his stupid mouth.

"You're obnoxious." I rolled my eyes.

"And you are incredibly worked up. How's that wine treating ya? Feeling nice and toasty yet, Matey?" he slurred, his grin growing lopsided.

"Excuse me?" I crossed my arms over my chest.

Heat flickered in the depths of his eyes. "Feeling toasty?

Ya know, warm all over." His drunken gaze searched my own. My breath hitched. "Like an animal in...*heat.*"

My cheeks warmed and my stomach churned. A knot formed in my lower belly. I narrowed my eyes. "The hell are you on about?" I gritted my teeth, our close proximity finally hitting me. We stood, less than an inch apart.

When did we—?

Husk danced in his words as his voice washed over me. "You know...the part of the brain that hates...has often been thought to intertwine with the part that signals...*lust.*"

My mouth went dry as my gaze slipped from his eyes, traveling to his kissable mouth. My tongue absentmindedly ran across my lips. "Ya don't say?"

Simon leaned in, his lips brushing against mine as he hummed a response, "Your move, Darling."

A thickness formed in my throat. Only a breath of air between us. I wanted, needed to tell the guy to fuck off. I had to.

But instead...my lips pressed against his. All the rage... irritation...bubbled to the surface, fueling the deepening lip lock.

His tongue darted out and I pulled it to mine, swirling, sucking. My teeth bit down on his lower lip and he groaned. My vision blurred as my eyes slid close, a haze of red flowed behind my eyelids. Something clawed its way through me, possessing me. My fist gripped his shirt and yanked him closer to me before shoving him backward onto the floor.

His pupils were blown and his chest was heaving. I planted one foot on each side of him, straddling him as I stood, towering over my prey. Simon lifted slightly, his elbows keeping him upright, waiting.

Good boy.

I dropped my hands to my sides and stepped between his legs, one foot landing just below his deliciously outlined hard on. I flicked it with the tip of my shoe, eliciting a satisfying whimper from him. "Nervous, Wolfie?" His Adam's apple bobbed as he swallowed thickly. I raised my other foot and pressed the heel of my tennis shoe to his chest, just above his beating heart. A smirk floated to my lips as a single bead of sweat dripped from his tousled titian hairline.

I leaned down, pressing my heel deeper into his chest. "Still think your little theory is true?" I smacked my lips.

I pushed him back, his spine colliding with the rug. "Because I'm really beginning to *loathe* you." I dug in, one final stab before I dropped to my knees.

I'm going to regret this when my buzz wears off.

Seven

SIMON

If this was a dream, I never wanted to wake up, because holy fucking shit.

Kali dropped to her knees with her still clothed center hovering over my strained cock. When the tip of her shoe connected with my chest, pressing into my flesh...my cum was on the verge of erupting from the head of my dick. It was torture having to restrain myself.

But I refused to be the one to make the first move. If she wanted this, even if it was a hot and heavy hate-fuck...I needed her to take the reins. I refused to cross that line. Taking wasn't my style.

Kali brought her hips down to mine, running the seam of her sweats against the outlined length of my cock. Her eyes fluttered as she ground against me, her arousal damp in the thick heated air between us.

Her hands slid up my chest, her long manicured nails digging in as she met the skin. I clenched my teeth, groaning, and she dug them in deeper, dragging them across my chest, the collar of my shirt moving and stretching as she went.

"Take it off," she commanded and I obliged, stripping the thing off with inhuman speed. Her eyes widened, surprised. The hatred in them faltered, her hunger taking over and she leaned forward until her breasts pressed against my chest, her hardened nipples poking through her shirt. She rubbed herself against me and began kissing my neck, then nipping and biting.

I moaned and my hands gripped the rug. It felt too good. *Too* good.

Fuck.

"No—" I huffed. "No biting. Not my neck."

She stopped, licking the spot she had been tending to before placing a singular deep kiss where I'd undoubtedly be sporting a winning hickey.

Kali's hips rocked again and I bucked against her, my strained cock rubbing her center, pulling a satisfying moan from her. She planted wet kisses down my chest, her tongue darting out once she reached my stomach, tracing each one of my visibly toned abs. I smirked as she continued, her mouth stopping at the waist band of my jeans. She glanced up, question in her eyes. I nodded and the blue poppies narrowed.

She was a predator and I...her willing prey.

My zipper was undone with expert precision and my cock sprung free, smacking her in the middle of her face.

"Fuck." She rubbed her nose. Then the hungriest smile I'd ever seen on a woman spread across her face. "I didn't realize you'd be so...*big.*"

I waggled my brows at her. "Think you can handle it, Princess?"

She licked her lips, her pupils widening. "Should ask yourself that, Wolfie."

And fuck did I.

Kali licked my shaft, agonizingly slow, until she reached the tip. Her tongue swirled around the tip, flicking it, sucking it, slurping up my pre-cum as it oozed from the center. She glanced up, mischief in her eyes, then swallowed me whole. Her lips wrapped, starving, around my pulsing dick, heavy with need, and took me down until she reached the base.

My soul was on the verge of being sucked out right there as she slid back up, releasing me with a beautiful pop.

"Fuck. You're perfect, Kali," I groaned. My head flung back as she went in for seconds, devouring me whole, over and over until I was on the edge. My dick twitched against her swirling tongue, ready to explode into her mouth.

"Ah, ah, Simon. No cumming until I say." Her sultry words dug their claws into my wolf. He howled in the back of my mind, begging for release.

"P-please, Kali," I whimpered.

She chuckled darkly.

Her palms moved up my chest, I felt her shift between my thighs. I glanced down to see her shimming out of her sweats.

How the fuck is she doing that?

Her finger tips pinched my nipple and I yelped.

"Eyes up here."

My gaze flicked back to hers. The warmth from one of her hands had disappeared from my chest.

I was too drunk on her to realize she'd removed it.

I'm royally fucked.

My head spun as I heard the distinct scuff of her sweats slipping over her thick, juicy never-skipped-a-leg-day-in-her-life ass. She wriggled between my legs then climbed on top of me, seating herself against my cock.

I started to move, needing to feel her juices coat me. She pinched me again.

"Who's in charge here, Simon?"

My voice was strangled. "You are."

She purred, "Good boy." Then I saw stars.

Kali slid her center along my dick, once, twice, then without warning, she slipped me between her wet folds, teasing me with just the tip. She swiveled her hips, wetting the head as she tested the waters. My body shook, my wolf clawing his way to the surface. Before I realized it, I tore through her tank, shredding to pieces.

I slipped my hand between us, pinching her clit, needing the distraction. She moaned, her body lurched and my cock burred itself in her sweet cunt.

Breathlessly, she moaned, "Oh. shit."

I smirked. "My turn." And I pounded into her as she braced herself against my chest. Her breasts bounced as her back arched with each thrust.

"Harder, please. Harder," she groaned.

I sat up and gripped her hips, ramming my cock deep inside her as I pulled her hips down in time with each of my thrusts.

Her nails clawed at my back as we fucked. Her chest pressed against mine as she rode me to oblivion.

She screamed, on the verge of unraveling and I spun her

around, easing her forward. Kali's face pressed against the rug, her hips lifted, fully displaying her ass and soaking cunt for me. Her hips waggled, begging.

I leaned forward, inhaling her arousal before dragging my tongue along her moist slit. Licking my lips, I growled into her cunt, the warmth of my breath causing her to shake. "Such a beautiful pussy. Drenched, just for me. What a dirty, dirty girl."

She panted, "Just for your cock. Not—not you."

I gently blew on her cunt and leaned back. "Is that so?" She whimpered at the distance. "I think you owe me an apology, human," I growled, letting my wolf fester, enjoying the sight in front of me. My mate, soaking wet, begging...for me. She squirmed, trying to press her thighs together for some friction. I gripped them, thrusting her succulent legs apart. She yelped at the cold breeze of the room as it hit her slit.

"I'm sorry!"

I leaned forward, covering her body with my own, just a hair away from our skin touching. "Say it."

"You—my pussy—it's all for you. All of you."

My palm rubbed along her ass, feeling her shutter at my touch. I pulled away, then landed a hard smack on her right cheek. She yelled out as her hips rocked. Then, she lifted her ass higher, ready for more. "Such a good little slut." She clenched as I brought my palm down on her cheek again, softly stroking her sensitive reddened skin. I bit each mark, following up with a planted kiss, rubbing her ass cheeks in between, massaging away the pain until she was ready.

Kali panted, drool dribbling from her parted lips. I lined the head of my cock up with her entrance, sticking just the tip in then dragging it along her slit until she couldn't take it anymore.

"For crying out loud. Fuck me already!" Her moans filled the air, the sweet sultry sounds clenching my hammering heart. "Please—I'm—begging—"

I shoved my dick between her folds before she could finish, all the way to the hilt. Thrusting in and out, I gripped her plump ass, squeezing, and rammed into her. Her moans echoed through the living room, merging with my own as we rode higher and higher until she was begging, groveling to cum.

"Not until I say," I grunted, mimicking her own words.

"Fuck—you!"

I smirked and bent forward, our bodies slapping together as we neared our peaks. "Lucky for you, Princess." I paused at her entrance, building to the finale. "Because Simon says...Cum." I buried my cock deep with her, hitting the golden spot. She cried out as her orgasm crashed over her, her body shuttering as it moved through her.

I began to slide out of her, until her walls clenched around me, locking me in.

Oh fuck.

I tried to pull out before it happened but failed miserably as my knot swelled. Kali's body twitched around me and my seed shot out, filling her until it seeped out her pussy, with it my cock.

I leaned against her, my arms wrapped around her waist as we slid to the floor. Brushing her hair from her face, I whispered my sorrys over and over, quietly sobbing until my throat screamed in pain.

There was no going back now.

Eight

KALI

My head was pounding. A dumbbell straight to the skull and on the verge of splitting in two. The pain dragged a mangled groan from my throat.

Too much wine.

I rolled over onto my side. A warm breeze caressed my face and I sighed. Earth, musk, and a hint of nutmeg settled into my bones.

Mmm...

There was a pull at my stomach, circling my waist. My body was tugged forward until it met the heated length of bare skin. Bare, chiseled skin.

Alek?

No, that couldn't be right. I was at Maeli's last night with her, Alastor, and that tool.

Wait.

Oh, no.

Oh, NO.

My eyes shot open. Simon's stupid face laid right in

front of me. His mouth parted and a heavy intake of air stroked a nasally snore from his airways.

Shit shit shit.

I scrambled out of his sleep-induced trap, scuttling to the opposite end of the living room once I was free.

My chest heaved.

I slept with Simon.

Not even.

I banged the ever-*loathing* shit out of him.

What the actual *hell* was I thinking?

Fucking shit.

I gotta get out of here. If he wakes up...fuck.

My feet tripped over each other as I struggled to get up, my legs screaming at me. My insides twisted and knotted, sending a wave of nausea raking through me. Everything from the middle of the night hate-and-bangathon soared through my mind, replaying each minute detail. Every moan, groan, command. They all rang in my ears. A thundering quickly followed. Frantically, my attention flicked around the room trying to figure out the source. Then I glanced down. My chest. The thundering was my pulsing heart. Blood raced through my veins, pumping into overdrive.

Stay. Stay. Stay.

Panic seized my insides. A cry.

What the fuck is happening?

This isn't right.

I need to go. I can't...

Something within me cried out, again.

Stay. Stay. Stay.

I jumped as another snore tore itself from Simon's drooling mouth.

Nope.

I scurried to my feet, clambering across Maeli's living room as I sprinted around, trying to gather all my clothes. I cursed myself when I caught a brief sight of my ripped tank top. I left it where it was splayed and reached for my hoodie, yanking it over my undoubtedly sex-crazed floor head before jumping into my visibly stained sweatpants. The sweet and salty tang of cum stung my nose.

Those were getting tossed in a tub of bleach when I got home.

I snatched my keys off the counter in Maeli's kitchen and turned around to rush my ass out of there.

"Forgetting something?" Simon mused, the heaviness of sleep clinging to his voice.

I whipped around, keys in a death grip in one hand, while my fingers twitched on the other. My startled, crazed line of sight landed on my phone, loosely dangling from between his thumb and forefinger...the very ones he used on a different button...

No, focus.

Fuckboy here is the enemy. Not a bang buddy.

"Give me my phone," I ground out between my clenched teeth.

He gave me a lopsided grin. "Awe, is that how you talk to someone you just fucked?"

I lurched forward, reaching for my screen.

He lifted it higher and clicked his tongue. "My, my, little Kali. Where are your manners?"

I snarled, clenching my fist. "I'll show you fucking *manners*, asshole. Give. Me. My. Phone."

He glanced up, tapping his chin. "Hmmm...I don't know. Maybe if you say pretty please."

I gritted my teeth.

"Simon, that's not the way to treat a lady. Give Kali her phone," Alastor said as he walked in, clearly coming from his and Maeli's room. "And while you're at it, please clothe yourself. Seeing another man's penis isn't on my to-do list for the day."

Simon glanced down, apparently forgetting he was buck ass naked. Before I could stop myself, I glanced down and immediately regretted it because saliva pooled in my mouth as I took in the hard beauty that was this asshole's dick.

Get a damn hold of yourself, Kali. You're better than this.

I tore my attention from it, only to find him looking at me, with a stupid satisfied smirk plastered on his face.

I scoffed and snatched my phone from his distracted hand. Turning on my heel, I waved over my shoulder, thanking Alastor. "Tell Maeli I'll call her later."

"Will do, be safe heading home."

Simon's lips smacked together, obnoxiously smooching the air behind me. "What, no kiss?"

I closed my eyes and sucked in a steadying breath. "Go fuck yourself."

An audible thunk followed me out the door. Alastor had smacked him on the back of his head.

Good.

I walked the path from the hidden cottage, through the

woods, and to the main road. The hair on the back of my neck stood on end. As if I were being watched.

I shook the feeling. I was striding through an animal filled forest, even if it was near the edge. Of course, I'd feel their beady eyes on me.

After a few minutes, I hit the paved sidewalk and turned toward home, glad I'd had the sense to don one of my heavier hoodies before I'd gone to Maeli's. The moment I got to Main St., a brisk, bone-chilling wind swept by, its icey tendrils assaulting the exposed part of my face. I hurried along the final stretch to home, kicking it up to a solid run as the front stoop came into sight.

I stopped, beeping my key card on the pad and shuffling inside. I hustled up the steps to my second floor apartment and shoved my key into the doorknob. Once it clicked, I turned the latch and stepped inside, immediately making a beeline for my shower. I stripped off my clothes, tossed them in the spare hamper on the opposite side of the bathroom, and dropped my phone on top of the vanity. I set the shower to boiling and hopped in, letting the gloriously hot water flow over my naked body. The grated nerves and wrenching panic that had lingered fell away, gradually replaced with waves of calming pleasure.

I let out a contented sigh, the more delightful, less hatedrenched parts of the day, before rising to the surface. A book deal. With my dream publisher. It was a dream come true. My books were going to be on shelves everywhere. I'd be on tour and traveling across the country, maybe even the world.

A smile spread across my face.

Finally, after busting my ass for so freaking long. It was

happening. New doors were being unlocked. I'd be able to do the things I wanted to do, see places I'd only ever dreamed of. Have the life I wanted, the one I'd fought for.

The one I'd left home for.

I stopped myself. I was not about to ruin a perfect scorching shower by going *there*.

Nope. Bad thoughts belonged in the outside world. Not in my steamy sanctuary.

I lathered away the threatening memories, massaging the minty shampoo into my scalp then rinsing it through with the detachable shower head. I moved the beating water across my skin, washing away the grim, the scent of that asswipe's delicious...hot...

Fucking dammit.

Heat flooded my system, my skin growing sensitive as Simon's moans filled my ears. He was a fucking dick.

But oh my god...he was...hot. And fucked like a maniac.

My cheeks flushed as need pooled in the pit of my stomach. I panted as the hot water from the shower beat against my increasingly sensitive skin. I traced my fingertips along my collar bone, slowly edging south. Caressing my breast with my palm, I began massaging, fondling the soft tissue behind my hand, stroking and pinching my taut peak as I went. With my other hand, the shower head ascended, gliding up my body until I reached my chest. I switched the settings, increasing the intensity of the water and dragged it downward until the pounding liquid met my wet center. A moan erupted from my throat and my other hand shot down, abandoning my breasts, and dove into my folds. One, two, then three fingers glided into my wetness.

Swirling them around with precision, I scraped the

sensitive spot inside, causing my legs to shake, the tension already coiling in the pit of my stomach. My chest heaved as I panted in time with my ministrations. I slipped to the floor, the shower head falling to the side, forgotten as I picked up speed, pumping my fingers in and out of myself. My thumb circled the bundle of nerves begging for friction. I pressed against my clit, sending me further into a frenzy. My body shook as my climax hit, shattering me from the inside out. I sped up, following the wave through until my muscles couldn't take any more and gave out completely.

I slumped against the shower wall, gasping for breath.

Never had I cum that quickly by only my hand. Usually, toys of all kinds were needed for me to get the job done.

Holy shit.

"What...is...happening...to...me..." I panted, my lids growing heavy by the second.

Simon's stupid face flashed behind my eyes.

Blood rushed through my veins and the sated pleasure-induced exhaustion evaporated. I was racked with another uncontrollable wave, as if the orgasm from the big guy upstairs hadn't just consumed me.

I groaned, not able to fight it, and started strumming the humming strings again until another unbelievable orgasm crashed into me. Then again. And again. Every time I felt like I was sated, the hunger roared again, re-energizing me until I came, covering my shower floor.

I was on the brink of passing out, my vision blurring and body shaking from all the spasms. I let my eyelids slide close, grateful that the water had finally cooled as it pelted my overheated skin. Sleep whispered to me, coaxing me into unconsciousness when a muted knock pulled me from the cliff. My eyes fluttered before closing again.

Just...hearing...things.

Fog filled my brain as my thoughts muddled.

I faintly registered a crash from the other room. My brows furrowed.

Imagining...things...

A comforting warmth wrapped around me, lifting me and guiding me as I floated through the air.

Quiet touches whispered across my cheeks, gliding along my tired skin.

"Kali..."

Something in me stirred, an exhausted rumble spread through me, splintering across my overused anatomy.

Softness brushed across my forehead. "Babe..." The velvety whisper of an angel. "I'm so sorry."

I tried to move my lips, to no avail. Tell the angel there was nothing to apologize for. But I was too weak, too spent.

So, instead, I let my mind drift off. Sleep quickly welcomed me into its pale, muscular earth-scented arms.

Nine

SIMON

I fucked up.

I fucked up so damn bad.

Stupid stupid stupid.

Why did I have to go and be a flirtatious asshole and send her running?

Now, she's suffering because of me.

Well...kinda.

Uncontrollable hot-for-wolf syndrome wasn't too bad. Unless the human hit with the bangarang gene happened to *hate* their mate.

Which Kali did. And Gods could only tell what she was going to do to me once she found out.

My foot tapped relentlessly as all the horrors marathoned through my brain. Her kicking my ass. Convincing Maeli to gut me, or Alastor. Then when they weren't looking, chopping off my beautiful cock to use as a dildo. Somehow getting some witchy magic shit so it wouldn't decay with the rest of me.

Actually, that might not be too bad.

Wait.

I'd be dead.

I shook my head.

Maybe she'd make a rug from my wolf pelt and parade me around like an actual dog. I shivered at that one. As a wolf shifter...that would possibly be the worst thing a human could do to one of us.

"Gods fucking dammit," I swore under my breath.

I gotta tell her.

When she wakes up...I gotta tell her and save my precious fur.

I glanced down at the sleeping woman next to me, her chest rising and falling with every breath.

I hung my head. "I'm so sorry, Kali. If I wasn't so—"

Her comforter swished as she began to stir. I froze, waiting. Her head turned and her eyes fluttered open. Confusion furrowed into the subtle lines on her face. "What... Simon?" She blinked.

Then shot out of bed. "What the fuck are you doing in my apartment? In my fucking *room*?"

I held my hands in front of me. "Just...I can explain."

Her head swiveled and she reached for her bedside lamp, snapping the cord as she wrenched it from its spot on her nightstand. "Get the fuck out!" she howled and swung. I dove off her bed, narrowly avoiding the metal rod, and landed on my stomach with a thud.

She clambered over her mattress, threats rambling as she came after me, the promise of my death in her fiery eyes. "I'm going to gut you, you fucking creep!"

Scrambling to my feet, I bolted out of her bedroom door and toward the kitchen. The lamp went flying by my head and I grabbed the first thing in my reach. Turning back to my seriously pissed off mate, I flipped the switch and her faucet blew, drenching her in lukewarm water from the kitchen sink.

That stopped her in her tracks. Her mouth fell open, stumped. The shock wore off quicker than I'd hoped. "Did you seriously just *spray* me? Do I look like a freaking *cat* to you!?"

I spritzed her again. "Well, considering cats aren't really my type, I'm going with no."

She screamed and threw herself at me. Her foot connected with my chest, knocking me back and wooshing the air out of my lungs.

Fuck, she packs a punch. Hot.

She swung around, roundhousing me and took me to the ground. My head banged against the linoleum floor. Stars spun, circling my throbbing head as my vision blurred. A groan slipped from my throat.

"How the hell did you get in here?" She stood over me, her knee digging into my collar bone, threatening to move up and crush my windpipe.

I coughed. "Woah, there, Lady."

Her knee moved north, pressing into my neck. "Tell. Me. Or Alastor is going to wake up to a wolf corpse at their doorstep tomorrow."

I tried swallowing and ended up choking on my own spit, my airway slightly restricted from the pressure.

The bastard wouldn't get rid of my body without a

word to Maeli. I know he would tell her. And so did she. But I wasn't about to call her bluff. Not in the very delicate position I found myself in.

Especially if I wanted to hide the pitched tent just out of her line of sight. I'd *really* be a dead wolf then.

Maybe she'd play mercy on me for it.

The corner of my lips twitched and her eyes narrowed.

Okay. Maybe not.

"I picked the lock." I sucked in a strangled breath. "I-I got worried." More pressure. Although I wasn't sure where it was worse...my throat or in my jeans. "Your heart rate was all over the place—"

I swore her pupils slit. "My *heart rate*? Are you on some type of doggy cat-nip?"

"No! Just...let me up. Please, Kali, I'll tell you everything."

She chewed her lip, mewling it over before finally easing off my neck. "Fine. But if you so much as step a toe out of line, I'm gutting you."

I strained as I fought the eye roll threatening to make an appearance.

She leaned back on her heels before standing, cautiously stepping backward and around her kitchen counter, never taking her eyes off of me.

Not putting her back to me. Smart.

She stood, waiting for me to follow.

I hopped up, dusting myself off, and strode to join her. Making myself comfortable, I plopped down onto her love seat, with my feet propped on her large coffee table. I patted the open seat next to me and flashed her a smile. "Might want to take a seat, Sweetheart."

Kali crossed her arms and jutted her hip out to her side. "Yeah, I think I'll pass, Dickwad."

I shrugged. "Suit yourself." I sighed, my finger tapping against the plush armrest. "Where to start. Where. To. Start...Ah, yes. That whole fingerbanging yourself until you passed out? Yeah...that's kinda my fault. Well, *our* fault, really. You see, shifters have these crazy connections called mates—"

"Yeah, thanks Captain Dog Brain. Maeli and Alastor filled me in on their whole supernatural mumbo jumbo."

I held up my finger, waggling it. "You've heard the panther's situation. Not mine." Pausing for dramatic effect, I rubbed my thumb and forefinger together until the irritated tap of Kali's heel told me it'd been long enough. "You see, for me, my fated mate, although not rare...is a bit more complicated."

Mostly because we didn't know jack squat about the witch shifter thing since as far as we knew, it had never happened before. But that was neither here nor there.

I continued, "My mate...the bond can be broken. Except if there was a knot in place. Once that happens... they're kinda stuck, literally and figuratively."

"So, what does this have to do with me?" She placed her hands on her hips.

I arched my brow. "No question on what a knot is?"

"Author, remember?" she deadpanned.

"Good point." A light bulb went off in my head. I flashed her a smile, "Actually, *a very* good point. That little shifter romance you wrote—"

Her cheeks flushed. "How do you know about—"

"Hey, I read from time to time." It was a lie but she

didn't need to know that. "Anywho, right on the money, *Mate-y*."

She rolled her eyes. "Oh my fuck, will you stop it with the—" Her eyes widened.

Bingo.

"No. You can't be serious." Blood drained from her face. "It's...no. You're fucking with me. You're just some psycho creep trying to get in my head."

"Twenty-two times," I blurted.

"I—what?"

"Twenty-two times. That's how many weirdly earth-shattering orgasms you had yesterday, right?"

She froze. "How did—"

I leaned forward, my elbows propped on my knees. "I felt every. Single. One. The only difference is I have pure wolf stamina on my side. Versus you...are human."

Kali's mouth clamped shut.

"And when we did the drunken tango...unfortunately, with your tight little pussy clenched around my cock, my knot took hold and I couldn't get out in time. So—"

"You fucking *knotted* in me? Are you fucking kidding me?" The calmness was eerie as she looked at me, the gears in her head churning.

"I—"

"You fucking trapped me in some sick supernatural relationship with you?"

"I'm sorry, Kali. Look, we don't have to date or even be a couple. But there's—"

The air became arctic.

"I. Hate. You."

"We can fix it—"

"I. HATE. YOU," she yelled. "Get the hell out of my apartment before I call the cops and have you arrested."

"Dammit, Kali! *I can't leave you.*"

"To hell you can't—"

I growled, getting to my feet, "You wanna collapse like that again?"

She stopped. "Excuse me?"

"If I leave, and we're not around each other, it'll happen again. It'll keep happening unless I'm with you. Unfortunately, it's some type of fucked up fail-safe between wolfs and their mates."

Her eyes narrowed. "Then explain to me how Maeli doesn't go through this. Because right now, it sounds like some sorry ass excuse to keep me in your clutches."

"It's a wolf thing. Other shifters, as far as we know, don't deal with this shit if they end up with a human mate."

"Isn't that fucking convenient," Kali scoffed.

"If that's your idea of convenient, then sure." I pinched the bridge of my nose. "You really think I want to be tied to someone who hates me for the rest of my life?"

Regardless of how beautiful she was.

She gave me an up-down glance. "I'm sorry, am I supposed to be *grateful?* Because you're fucking dreaming if you think that's going to happen."

My eyes rolled. "Not even in the slightest. But a little less of a bitchy attitude would be nice."

Ice laced her laugh. "Tough titties, Asswipe."

I smirked and her phone came flying toward my head. Ducking out of the way, I snatched the thing and twirled it between my fingers. "Actually, if I remember correctly, they were pretty soft."

"You're disgusting."

Shrugging, I shoved the screen into my back pocket, then hooked my thumbs through my belt loops at the front of my jeans. "Yeap." Clicking my tongue, I glanced around. It was the first time I'd been here in the morning. Well, that Kali knew of at least.

Oh, she'd definitely kick my ass if she found out now.

Might be fun.

I snuck a quick glance. She was stewing.

Maybe not.

Kali fisted her hands, "Give me my phone back."

I quirked my brow, then stepped around the coffee table and toward her front door. I threw my hand over my shoulder as I stepped out to the hall. "Nah, not feelin' it. Could go for some grub, though."

A shoe whistled through the air, missing me by a whole foot and hitting the door across the hall.

Good thing she doesn't have any neighbors yet.

"Give it back!"

"Buy my breakfast and you can have it," I said over my shoulder.

Kali mumbled a slew of curses before adding a tight lipped, "Fine."

"Oh, and by the way, we'll stop by my place and grab a few things since I'll have to stay here til we get this figured out."

"WHAT?"

"I'll meetcha downstairs, *Mate*," I said with a smile, my

back still to her as I hurried down the stairs before she could throw anything else at me.

The wild yelling followed me out, even audible from the front stoop.

"*Really* dug myself in it now."

My wolf practically paraded around my skull. My grin widened.

We're hopeless.

Ten

KALI

My life...was fucking over.

My love life, at least.

I was eternally tied to some jerk-faced creep.

With zero say in the matter.

No warning.

That's what I fucking get for hate-fucking some douche bag.

A cute douche bag.

A dickliciously cute douche bag.

Kali Merry, get a damn hold of yourself.

I would not fall for some asshole just because some supernatural mumbo jumbo said so. Fuck that shit.

Unbreakable my ass.

I'd find a way out of this, and when I did, I'd be sending that wolf packing.

"I'll have to stay here til we get this figured out." My ass.

My eyes rolled as I stood, pissed to all hell on the sidewalk outside of Simon's place. It was a small single story on the opposite end of town. The outside was starting to crumble. Windows cracked, a couple were even broken completely, glass fragments the only sign that there had been one there in the first place. The door loosely hung from its hinge and creaked loud as hell when Simon had gone through it.

I couldn't believe he lived like that.

The poor thing.

I shook my head.

No, he's a jackass. Don't sympathize with the enemy, Kali.

Besides, the jerk wouldn't let me inside. So, for all I knew, it could be a front. Some dumb disguise to keep shitty people out.

But who would be stupid enough to steal from a wolf?

I squeezed my eyes shut and counted to ten. My mind was all jumbled and overstimulated from the hellish day and information overload.

I was physically and emotionally exhausted.

And as for how I've been acting...I haven't been myself. It was like every part of me was just *on edge.*

I was sick and tired of it.

A crunch from behind lulled me from my thoughts. I whipped my head around, ready to run.

"Thanks for waiting, didn't mean to take so long." I let out a breath, it was only Simon.

'Only' Simon.

I scoffed at myself.

He gave me a weird look before he turned on his heel, heading back the way we came. "You coming?"

"Yeah, yeah. Just...not what I was expecting." I floundered, falling in step with him.

He tossed his bag over his shoulder and stuffed his other hand in his jacket. "Ha, sorry to disappoint. No penthouse for this stud." His laugh was hollowed. "Its not much, but its mine. Or it was."

My brows furrowed. "What do you mean?"

"The place is getting torn down here in a few weeks. Got condemned."

My forehead creased as my brows shot sky high. "Can they even do that?" My blood boiled. I didn't like the guy, but he shouldn't lose his place just because it's a little run down.

Okay, very run down.

The place would probably blow over with a slight breeze.

"They can when the owners are gone." He sniffed the air, glancing around before we crossed the road. "My parents passed away a while ago. It was theirs."

"Oh..."

"Yeah, it is what it is. Happens all the time in Shifterland. Mine just so happened to live among the humans."

"You didn't?"

Why am I keeping this up?

His personal life is none of my business. I don't care.

Shouldn't care.

This mate shit is a hoax. Breakable.

Stupid and doesn't matter...

It didn't matter. None of it did.

Something in me shifted.

But...maybe it did.

"Human's weren't really my shtick. Most of them were

assholes. But my parents thought otherwise. So, when they decided to move out here, I left. Didn't talk to them for a long time. Then one day, got a call from one of the others. They were gone." He shifted his bag to the other shoulder. "Later found out, the one who called me was the wolf who did it. He worked for Bitch-eena. She wanted them murdered because they were 'human sympathizers.' What you saw was how they left the place after gutting my parents."

Shit. Here I thought my stuff was rough.

"I'm sorry, Simon."

He stopped. I took a few steps, expecting him to follow but he didn't. I turned, and he stood there in the middle of the sidewalk, his face stone cold. "You're sorry? For what? My parents being gone? For not knowing where I've been living? Or the fact that the best sleep I've had in weeks has been outside your fucking window? Or for fucking my brains out then giving me the cold shoulder?"

"You *what*?"

"You heard me."

A furious bone-chilling calm fell over me. "You've been sleeping outside my window? Without me knowing? Invading *my* personal space?"

"Yeah, I have. And guess what? I'd do it again, Princess."

"Stop calling me that you fucking weirdo."

"Make me, *Princess.*"

"Go to hell, Simon," I growled, my body shaking.

He laughed, arctic air on his breath. "My mate rejecting me? I'm already there, Sweetheart."

HAVE A NAUGHTY NEW YEAR

Shiftmas Book Three
End

Acknowledgments

Thank you to my husband for all the support and encouragement. I also want to give a huge thanks to my street team, editor, readers, fellow authors, and the book community. This has been such a fun series to write! I've loved seeing so many readers enjoying this mini series and am excited to continue Maeli and Alastor's journey along with Simon and Kali!

Also by S. P. Icey

A Series of Smutacular Witchy Shifter Novellas

Have A Holly Jolly Shiftmas (Book One)

Have A Witchin' Howl-O-Ween (Book Two)

Standalone's

Suck Me Harder: A Smutty Vampire Romance Novella

www.ingramcontent.com/pod-product-compliance
Lightning Source LLC
Chambersburg PA
CBHW042034120726

47911CB00027B/732